**Welcome to the Worl**
**With the help of this great**
       **amazing magnets** ...

## INCLUDED IN YOUR KIT:

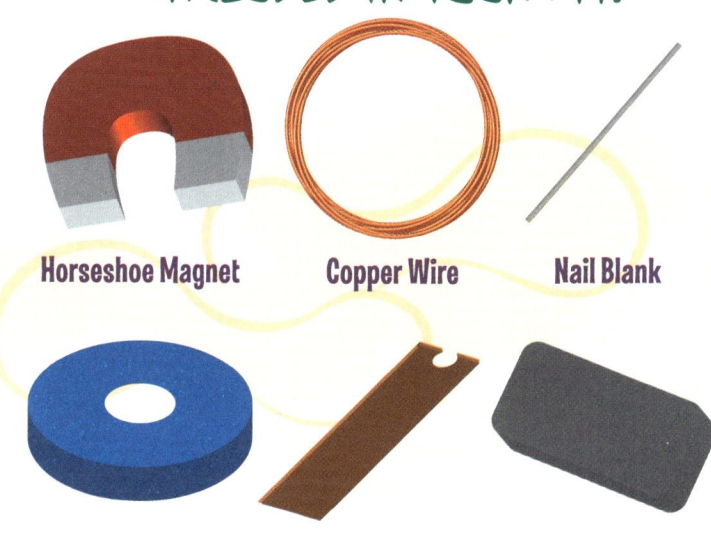

**Horseshoe Magnet**   **Copper Wire**   **Nail Blank**

**2 Ring Magnets**   **2 Motor Mounts**   **2 Bar Magnets**

Written by Jo Hurley
Designed and Illustrated by Marty Baumann, Bill Henderson, and Deena Fleming.
All rights reserved. No part of this publication may be reproduced, or stored in a retrieval system, or transmitted in any form, or by any means, electronic, mechanical, photocopying, recording, or otherwise, without written permission of Tangerine Press.
Copyright © 2005 Scholastic Inc.
Scholastic and Tangerine Press and associated logos are trademarks of Scholastic Inc.
Published by Tangerine Press, an imprint of Scholastic Inc; 557 Broadway; New York, NY 10012
ISBN 0-439-55127-7
Printed in China

Scholastic Canada              Scholastic New Zealand              Scholastic Australia
Markham, Ontario               Greenmount, Auckland                Gosford, NSW

# BACK TO BASICS

## LONG, LONG AGO, IN A PLACE FAR, FAR AWAY ...

People have known about magnets ever since the time of Ancient Greece... more than a thousand years ago! The Ancient Greeks discovered stone that stuck to pieces of iron. Whoa, magic! They called the stones lodestones, or magnetite. Researchers believe the word "magnet" comes from Magnesia, a part of Ancient Greece.

"So, you want to know what magnets are all about? Hey, you think I became a world-renowned magnet expert just by reading page four? Okay, maybe I did."

## NOT SO LONG AGO...

Scientists have learned some weird stuff about "magic" magnets. For one thing — one big thing — they're not magical at all. They also figured out:

- **Magnets attract metals made of iron.**
- **Magnets have north and south poles.**
- **Magnets are surrounded by invisible fields of force.**
- **Magnetism and electricity are somehow connected.**

## Safety First

1. Don't drop the magnets. They can break and chip. It can also weaken the strength of the magnet.
2. Wear safety goggles in case a magnet breaks during an experiment.
3. Don't snap magnets together. They could break or chip. Let magnets come together slowly, so they don't pinch your fingers.
4. Throw out any pieces of a broken magnet.
5. Don't put magnets near a TV, computer, credit card, computer disk, or video or audio tape. They can really mess them up.
6. Be very careful using batteries and wire in the experiments. The wire can get hot and batteries can leak. If you use more than one battery at a time, do not mix different types batteries and do not mix old and new batteries. If the wire gets hot, let it cool before you touch it.

**Always have an adult help with experiments that use batteries or wire. Besides, they may learn something!**

# STICK TO IT

Okay, let's start off with an easy experiment. You've probably seen magnets in action, so you probably know that they stick to some things – and not to others. But what's the difference? Here's how to figure it out.

**YOU NEED:**
- **Magnet**
- **Household objects (like a paper clip, chalk, pen, tin can, eraser, safety pin, coin or toothpick).**

1. Collect a bunch of small objects from around your house. Try to choose things that are made of different materials.
2. Hold each object up to your magnet. Does your magnet have any effect on it?
3. Now, make two piles: objects your magnet sticks to, and objects your magnet does not stick to. Do you notice anything about the objects in these two piles? Can you predict what kind of objects will stick to your magnet?

## RULES OF ATTRACTION

Most of the objects that magnets attract are made out of iron. Objects that are attracted by magnets are called ferromagnetic.

## WARNING:

Keep your magnets away from electronic devices, videotapes, audio tapes, and computer disks.

"TURN TO PAGE 27 TO SEE WHY MAGNETS CAN DO MAJOR DAMAGE."

**MEGA MAGNET CHALLENGE!**

Not all magnets are created equal. How many paper clips can you pick up with each magnet? Can you find your strongest magnet?

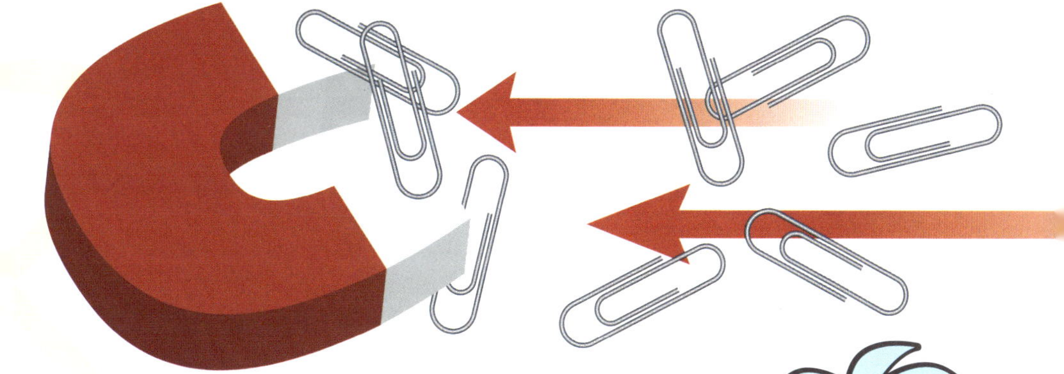

# MAGIC MOTION

Bring your magnet very close to a paper clip, without touching it. What happens? The paper clip will move on its own, as if an invisible force is drawing it toward the magnet.

## YOU NEED:
- Magnet (any shape)
- 5 paper clips
- Piece of paper
- Piece of cardboard
- Sheet of aluminum foil

1. Put 5 paper clips on a piece of paper.
2. Carefully lift the paper, keeping the paper clips on top of it.
3. With your other hand, touch the magnet to the bottom of the paper, directly under the paper clips.
4. Rub the bottom of the paper with the magnet. When you move the magnet, do the paper clips move, too? If they do, that means the magnetic force can act through the paper.
5. Try this experiment with other materials. Can the magnetic force act through aluminum foil? How about through plastic? Glass? Water?

Find the maze in your Super Science kit on page 38 and put a paper clip on top of it. Make the paper clip move by moving your bar magnet underneath the maze. How fast can you guide the paper clip through the maze? Once you've made it through the magnet maze, try making one of your own!

# MAKING MAGNETS

What makes a magnet a magnet? There's one easy way to find out: make one of your own!

**1.** Stroke the nail blank with one side of your bar magnet.

Stroke from the top to the bottom, about 100 times in the same direction.

With each new stroke, make sure you lift the magnet off the nail blank and start again at the top.

**2.** Touch the point of the nail blank to a paper clip. Does the nail blank act like a magnet? If not, try stroking it 50 more times.

**3.** How many paper clips can you lift with your magnetized nail blank? Is it as strong as your bar magnet? What happens when you shake the nail blank? Is it still magnetic?

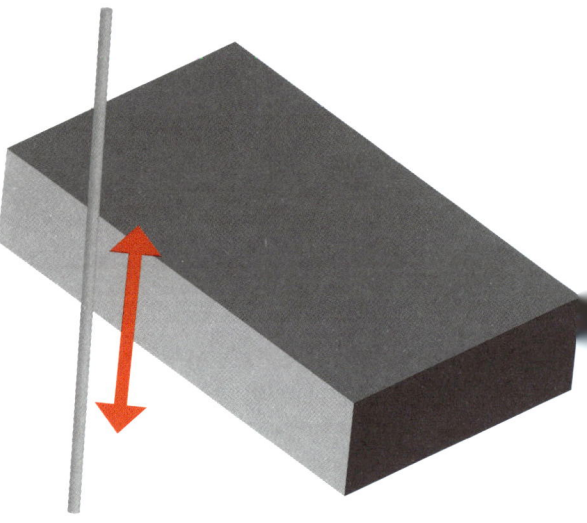

**YOU NEED:**
- **Nail blank (from kit)**
- **Bar magnet (from kit)**
- **Paper clip**

# MICROMAGNETS

Everything in the world is made up of millions and millions of atoms, tiny particles too small for you to see. Each atom creates a teeny magnetic force, called a *domain*.

In some materials, domains point in all different directions, so forces cancel each other out. This means these materials are NOT magnetic. But sometimes domains are all lined up the same way. These materials ARE magnetic.

By stroking the nail blank with your magnet, you made all its domains point in the same direction. Presto! The nail blank turned into a magnet. By shaking up the nail blank, you forced domains to point in different directions again. Poof! No more magnet.

- Does using different magnets change the strength of your magnetized nail blank?

- What happens if you stroke the nail blank 200 times, instead of 100 times? Does your nail blank become a stronger magnet?

- If you don't shake it, how long does the nail blank stay magnetic?

- What else can you magnetize? Try this experiment with other objects from around your house. Can you magnetize a nut or a bolt? A toothpick? How about a penny?

# FLOATING MAGNETS

So now we know your magnets can attract other objects.
Is that it? No way. Magnets can also push objects away, or repel them.

1. Lay both bar magnets on a table. Bring the side of one magnet near the end of another. What happens? Do they pull together (attract) or push apart (repel)?
2. If the magnets pull toward each other, turn one of the magnets around, and bring the opposite end toward the other magnet.
3. When you've found the ends of the magnet that repel, put a piece of masking tape on that end of each magnet.
4. Stack the magnets, so that the ends with the masking tape are directly on top of each other.
5. Stick a pencil in between the two magnets. Tape the magnets together, with the pencil in between them.
6. Now carefully slide the pencil out. There's nothing holding up the top magnet — it should just float in midair!

## YOU NEED:
- 2 bar magnets (from kit)
- Transparent tape
- Masking tape
- Pencil

## POLE POSITION

Every magnet has two poles, a north pole and a south pole. Opposite poles attract, and like poles repel. When the similar poles of your magnets came near each other, they pushed each other away. This made the top magnet "float."

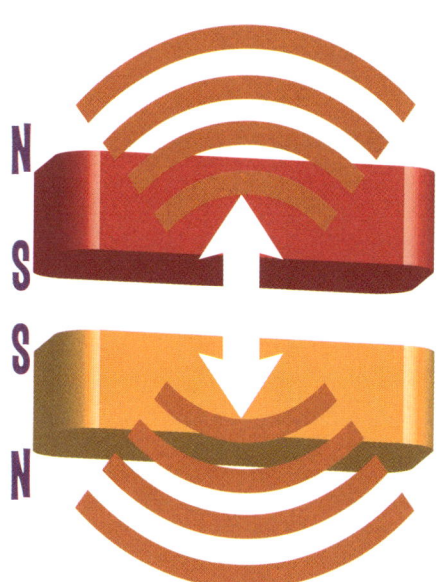

## MAGLEV MOTION

The same force that made your magnet float has been used by scientists to create the Maglev train. A magnetic track repels the magnetized train, so these trains actually levitate, or float, above the track! In 2000, a Maglev train broke the world train record, zooming above the tracks at 342 miles per hour!

# STRONG SPOTS

Different points on your magnet have different strengths. Can you find the strongest spots on each of your magnets?

**YOU NEED:**
- Magnets of different shapes and sizes
- Dish or bowl (not made of metal), should be bigger than your magnets
- 20 Paper clips
- 20" (50cm) of thread
- Transparent tape
- Pencil

1. Cut two pieces of thread. Each should be 10 inches (25cm) long.
2. Tie one end of the thread around a bar magnet, about half an inch from its end. Put a piece of tape over the thread to hold it in place.
3. Tie one end of the other thread around the other end of the bar magnet. Tape that in place, too.
4. Tie the other ends of the threads to a pencil, and tape them in place. Try your best to make the threads the same length, so that the bar magnet hangs horizontally (parallel with the ground).
5. Fill the bowl with paper clips.
6. Holding your pencil in the middle, dip the magnet into the bowl of paper clips.
7. Slowly lift it out of the bowl. Which parts of the magnet did the most paper clips stick to? These are the strongest points on your magnet.
8. Use the same technique to find the strong and weak spots on all your magnets.

## MEGA MAGNET CHALLENGE!

The most paper clips will always stick to the magnet's poles. The poles are in different places on differently shaped magnets. Your bar magnet's poles are on each side. Can you figure out where the poles are on your other magnets?

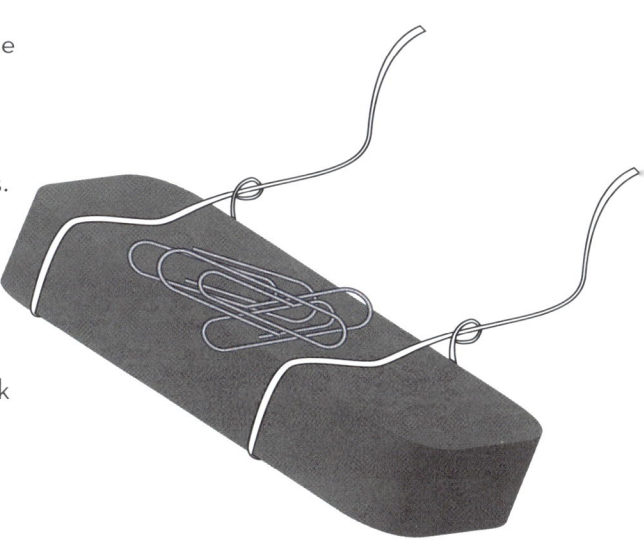

# PLANET MAGNET

What's the world's biggest magnet? Look down – you're standing on it! That's right, Earth is a magnet with its very own north and south poles. Scientists estimate that 1,800 miles (2,900 km) beneath your feet, Earth's core is surrounded by a layer of iron. This creates a mega-magnetic field that stretches into space for more than 100,000 miles (161,000 km)! Believe it or not, you can detect this big field with your own little magnets.

## YOU NEED:
- Magnet
- 2 metal wires made from unbending 2 paper clips
- Clear tape
- 20" (50cm) of thread
- Masking tape
- Compass

## WARNING:
Never let your magnet touch a compass. That can reverse the compass's polarity, which means that the compass would point in the wrong direction.

1. Magnetize both metal wires (see p. 8), so you have two wire magnets.
2. Stick one of your wire magnets onto a piece of tape.
3. Lay the thread across the tape, so that it makes a right angle with the wire magnet. Fold over the tape. The wire should now hang from the string horizontally (See Fig. A).
4. Stick a scrap of masking tape to one end of the second magnet wire. Bring that end near one end of the hanging magnet. What happens?
5. Since opposite poles repel, and like poles attract, figure out which ends of the wire magnets are like. Mark them with a scrap of tape.
6. Hang both wire magnets from separate strings using tape. Dangle them both – when they stop moving, are they both pointing in the same direction? If so, it means the like poles are both affected in the same way by the Earth's magnetic field.
7. Now you can find out which pole is which. Use your compass to find north. Which ends of your magnetic wires are pointing in that direction?

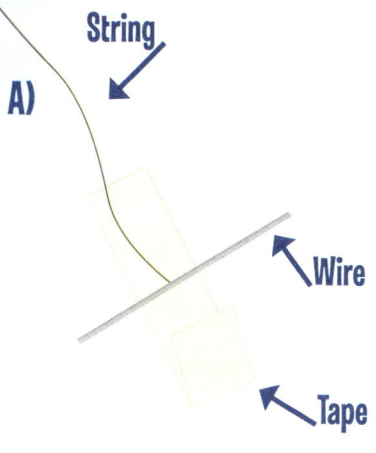

A) String
Wire
Tape

## USING A COMPASS

Hold the compass in the palm of your hand, and hold your hand very still until the needle stops moving. Now, with your other hand, gently turn the compass until the needle is pointing toward the spot labeled north. Now that your compass has shown you which way north is, you can figure out which direction you're facing. Try moving around the room, in all different directions, and watch what happens to the compass needle.

# FISH FRY

I know, I know, you've heard it all before. But did you know that there is a metal that is a liquid at room temperature? It's called mercury, like the planet, but different. This metal liquid can be found in small amounts in some fish. Mercury is magnetic, but I doubt you'd be able to pick up a real fish with a magnet. But, let's pretend you can. Find out which paper fish have pretend mercury in them by seeing if your magnet will pick them up.

**YOU NEED:**
- Circle magnet
- A pencil
- About 24 inches of string (it can be shorter)
- Paper fish (cut out about 20 of them)
- 10 Paper clips
- Scissors

**FISH TEMPLATE**

1. Trace the fish template provided, and use to cut out all 20 little fishies from construction paper. Ask your parents for help.
2. Tape a paper clip onto the back of ten fish.
3. Tie the end of the string around the pencil. This is your fishing pole.
4. Tie the other end of the string through the circle magnet.
5. Put all the paper fish on the floor. Make sure the paper clips are on the underside.
6. GO FISH!
    *Which fish does the magnet pick up?
    *What if you use smaller paper clips?
    *How close do you have to be to the fish for your fishing lure to pick up the fish?
    *How many fish can you pick up in one shot?

Okay, so you have the fishing pole idea. What about the Earth's poles? Earth's magnetic north pole is in the north—but that wasn't always the case. According to scientists, Earth's poles can flip-flop. This happened 700,000 years ago. Scientists think it may reverse again in a few thousand years—but they don't know why!

# COURSE CORRECTION

You've already seen that a magnetized paper clip will line itself up with the Earth's fields, just like a compass. So why not make a compass of your own! Here are two compasses that you can make yourself, with just a bar magnet and a few objects from around the house.

**YOU NEED:**
- Bowl (not metal)
- Water
- Bar magnet (from kit)
- Nail blank (from kit)
- Transparent tape
- 1/2" X 1/2" (2cm X 2cm) of flat Styrofoam, sponge, or cork
- Compass (or landmark that will help you find north)
- Marker

## FLOATING COMPASS

1. Fill the bowl halfway with water. Put it on a flat surface.
2. Follow the directions on p. 8 to magnetize a nail blank. Then test it with a paper clip, to make sure the nail is magnetized.
3. Tape the nail blank onto the Styrofoam, sponge, or cork. (Careful not to shake the nail – you don't want to de-magnetize it!)
4. Gently lay the Styrofoam on the surface of the water, nail blank side up. It should spin a bit, and the come to rest.
5. Use your compass to figure out which way is north. Is your nail blank pointing in that direction?
6. Note which end of your nail blank is pointing north. Carefully take the Styrofoam out of the water, and mark the correct side "north." Then mark the other sides east, south, and west.
7. Put the Styrofoam back in the water – and you've got a compass! Try gently spinning the Styrofoam around, and see what happens. Or move the bowl to another part of the room – does your nail continue to point north?

### THE FIRST COMPASS
The compass was invented in China several centuries ago – it first arrived in Europe in the 12th century.

# COURSE CORRECTION

## HANGING COMPASS

**YOU NEED:**
- Nail blank
- 10" (25cm) of thread
- Clear tape
- Straw
- Clear plastic cup (must be wider than the nail)
- Magnet
- Paper clip
- Masking tape
- Compass

1. Cut a notch on the rim of your cup. Now cut a notch on the opposite side.
2. Push your straw into the notch. Tape the straw in place.
3. Lay your nail blank across the middle of a piece of tape. Lay the end the thread on the tape too, perpendicular to the nail blank. Fold over the tape. The nail blank should hang horizontally from the thread.
4. Hold the nail blank by the tape. Magnetize one side of the nail (See Fig. B).
5. Gently lower the nail blank into the cup.
6. Tape the thread to the straw, so that the nail blank is dangling above the bottom of the cup (See Fig. A). Snip off any excess thread.
7. Use a compass to figure out which way north is. Put a small piece of masking tape on that end of the nail. Then lower it back into the cup. The nail is now free to swing toward north, no matter what. You've got your hanging compass!

A)

Straw

String

Nail

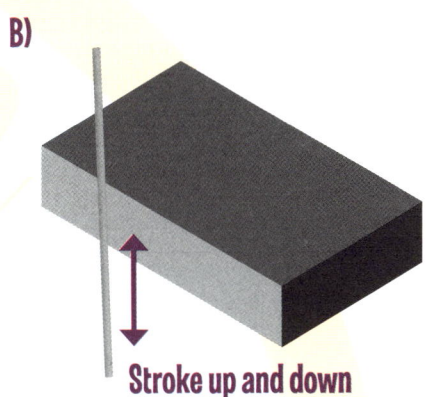

**B)**

**Stroke up and down**

## POLES ON THE MOVE

Unlike Earth's geographical north pole, the magnetic pole doesn't always stay in the same place. In fact, it can move 50 miles (80km) in one day! While the magnetic north pole is near the geographic North Pole, they're not in the exact same place. Fortunately, in most places on Earth, the distance between the two north poles is so small that it doesn't make much difference.

Some animals have built in compasses. Tiny magnetic crystals in their body, called magnetite, help them detect the Earth's magnetic field. Scientists have also discovered magnetite in the human brain. Does this mean that you can be a human compass? Scientists don't think so. Why not see for yourself? Hold a compass in your hand, close your eyes, and spin around. Can you tell which direction you're facing? Check the compass to see if you're right.

# GALVANOMETER

So now you know a lot more about magnetism than you did when you started. But that's not the whole story. Magnetism and electricity are connected—and here's how you can see electromagnetism, as the pair is called, in action.

## YOU NEED:
- Piece of cardboard 3 in. x 2 in. (7.5cm x 5cm)
- 20 in. (51cm) of copper wire in this kit
- Scissors
- Any battery
- Small piece of sandpaper
- Compass

1. Cut out the piece of cardboard 3 in. x 2 in. (7.5cm x 5cm). Make two cuts with scissors about 1/4-in. (1cm) into the cardboard. Space them about 3/4 in. (2cm) apart.
2. Use the sandpaper to scrape about 1-in. (2.5cm) off the coating on each end of the wire. Ask an adult to help you.
3. Place the compass in the middle of the cardboard rectangle.
4. Place the copper wire into one of the slits in the cardboard. Leave about 6 inches (15cm) of the wire before you start wrapping.
5. Wrap the copper wire around the cardboard and directly over the compass face.
6. End the wrap by putting the other end of the copper wire through the slot. This will leave you with two ends on the same side.
7. Now, let's test this baby! Hold one end of the copper wire to one end of the battery. Touch the other end of the wire to the other end of the battery. Watch the compass needle jump!

## WARNING

Always be careful and ask an adult for help when you're experimenting with electricity Never, <u>EVER</u> plug any of your experiments into a wall outlet! And watch out, because copper wire is a good conductor of electricity and does get hot!

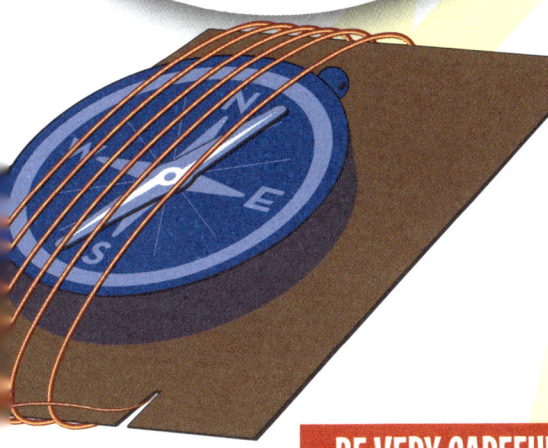

**BE VERY CAREFUL! THE COPPERWIRE WILL GET HOT! DO NOT LEAVE CONNECTED!**

## LAWS OF ELECTRO-FANTASTIC...MAGNETISM

A galvanometer is a device that detects and measures the flow of electricity. A simple galvanometer (like the one you made) is a compass with a wire wrapped around it. Connect the ends of the wire and it tests the battery for an electric current, which makes the needle jump. This is because the moving magnetic field is creating an electrical current in the wire. In the nineteenth century, scientists discovered this connection between electricity and magnetism. Now electricity and magnetism are treated as two parts of a single phenomenon: electromagnetism. Many of the devices you use every day, like motors, computers, doorbells, telephones, and tape recorders, just to name a few.

# FLOATING NAIL

So now you know that a moving magnetic field can create an electric current. Do you think an electric current can create a magnetic field? Why not...

## YOU NEED:
- 1.5 volt battery
- 20" (50cm) of copper wire (from kit)
- Drinking straw
- 8 Penny Nail (ask an adult)
- Transparent tape

1. Strip off about an inch (2.5cm) of insulation at each end of the wire. Ask an adult for help.
2. Tape one end of the wire to the positive battery terminal.
3. Wrap the wire around the drinking straw— make a coil that is a few layers thick.
4. Tape the coil of wire in place around the straw.
5. Tape the other end of the wire to the negative battery terminal.
6. Stick the nail inside the straw, and let go. What happens to the nail?

"COME ON, YOU'RE FAR ENOUGH ALONG IN THE BOOK TO FIGURE OUT WHAT COMES NEXT, RIGHT?"

## SOLENOID POWER

The nail should float inside the straw. The electric current winding around the straw has created a magnetic field, and the nail got trapped in it! In fact, whenever current travels through a wire, it creates a magnetic field around the wire. This is the principle of a solenoid.

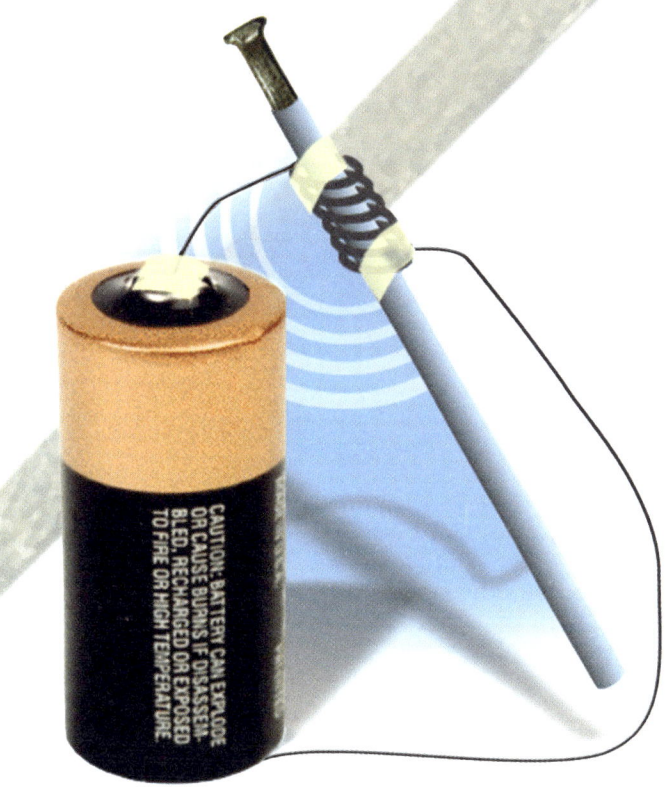

# ELECTROMAGNET

Now make this electromagnetic field work for you, by creating an electromagnet!

1. Strip off about an inch (2.5cm) of insulation at each end of the wire. Ask an adult for help.
2. Tape one end of the wire to one of the battery terminals.
3. Wrap the wire around the nail— make a coil that is a few layers thick.
4. Tape the other end of the wire to the other battery terminal.
5. Use your nail to pick up some paper clips—is the nail magnetic?
6. Remove one end of the wire from the battery. Will your nail still pick up paper clips?

## YOU NEED:
- 1.5 volt battery
- 20" (50cm) of copper wire (from kit)
- 8 penny nail (ask an adult)
- Transparent tape
- Paper clips

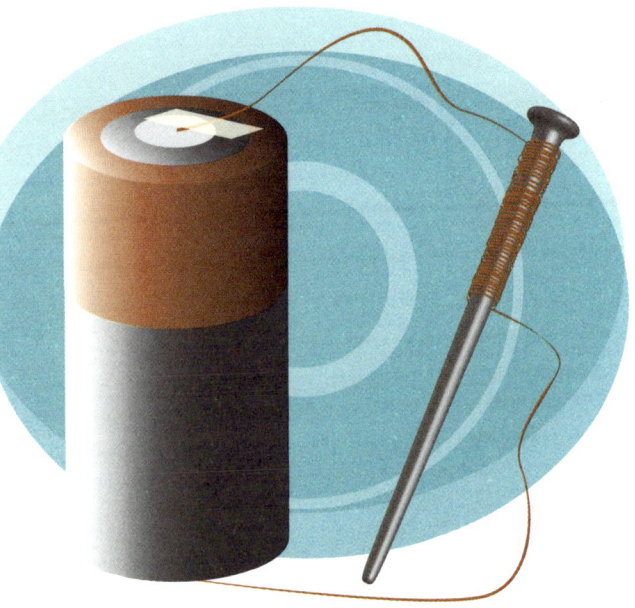

When electricity travels through a wire, a magnetic field forms around that wire. The electric current magnetized the nail, creating an electromagnet. When you removed the wire from the battery, you broke the current, and the nail no longer acted as a magnet.

*MEGA MAGNET CHALLENGE!*

## THAT'S ELECTRIFYING!

Motors aren't the only household items to make use of the connection between electricity and magnetism. Audio tapes, video tapes, and computer disks all translate electric signals into magnet ones, so they can store information on a magnetic strip. To see this for yourself, find a videotape or audiotape that you don't need anymore (be sure to check with your parents about this first!). Using a pencil or your finger, slowly rewind the tape. Rub a magnet along the strip of tape as it goes by. What happens when you play that tape? Rubbing the tape with a magnet disrupted the magnetic field and destroyed the information that was stored there.

# FLOATING MAGNET

It's magic! No, it's magnetic!

1. Place bar magnet #1 in the holder on the tray. Place the other magnet over it to determine which side repels.
2. Cut a 10-inch (25cm) piece of transparent tape and center over bar magnet #2.
3. Gently balance the magnet above the other magnet as high as possible.
4. Tape the ends to the tray.

**YOU NEED:**
- Tray (from kit)
- Two bar magnets
- Clear tape

## HOW DOES IT WORK?

MEGA MAGNET FACT!

Levitrons are special globes or toys that float using magnetic power.

Similar magnetic poles repel each other. So the top magnet appears to "float" above the bottom magnet. The tape holds the magnet in place.

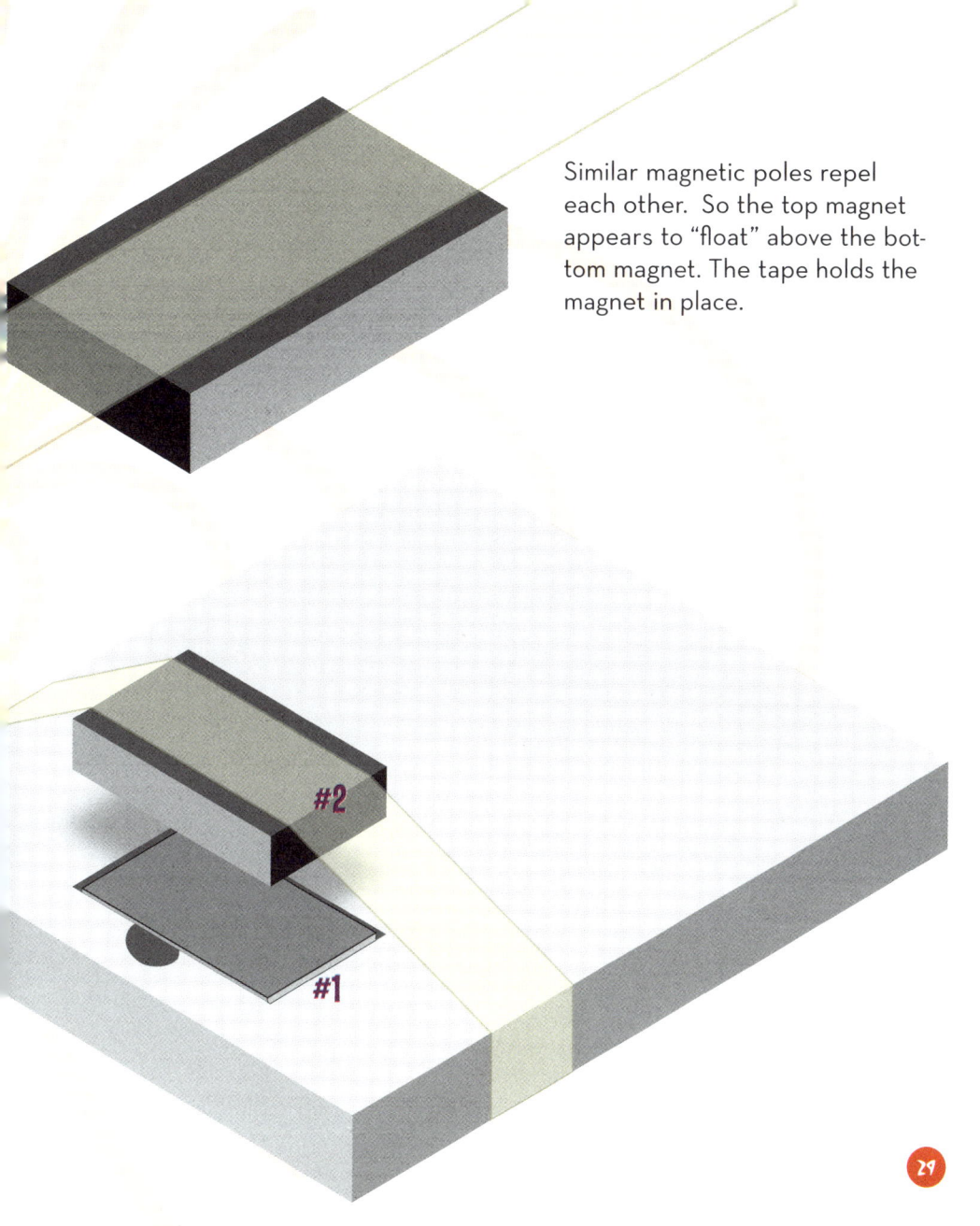

# ELECTRIC MOTOR

Amaze your friends with a wire that rotates by itself.

## YOU NEED:
- One "D" battery (or tube of similar size and shape)
- One "AA" battery
- Two copper motor mounts (from kit)
- One bar magnet (from kit)
- Copper wire (from kit)
- Fine sandpaper

1. Place the "AA" battery in the space provided in your tray.
2. Slide one copper motor mount into the tray so it touches one end of the battery. Do the same for the other mount.
3. Place the bar magnet over the center of the battery.
4. Now you need to make your coil of wire the correct shape. Leave about 3 inches (7.5cm) of wire, then wrap the remaining wire around the "D" battery (or similarly shaped object) to create a ring of wire. Leave another 3 inches (7.5cm) sticking out out from the other end as shown in figure A. Now wrap the two ends around the coil to hold it in place.
5. Place the ends of the coil in the grooves at the top of the motor mounts. Spin gently to make sure the coil is balanced. If it's unbalanced, re-align the ends.
6. Once the coil is balanced, remove it from the motor mounts. With a small piece of sandpaper, gently sand the top layer off one end half way around the wire.
7. Sand the bottom layer off the other end the same way.
8. Place the coil back into the grooves of the motor mount and gently spin the coil. If it doesn't spin by itself, try spinning it in the other direction. It only works in one direction.

A)

Wrap

## TROUBLESHOOTING TIPS

Sanding the correct amount of insulation off of the wire is very important. If your motor won't spin, sand a little more insulation off. You can take up to two-thirds of the insulation off. DO NOT SAND OFF ALL THE INSULATION AROUND THE WIRE ON THE ENDS—the motor will not work!

**NOTE:** If you scraped off the ends of the wire for a different experiment, snip off the scraped ends.

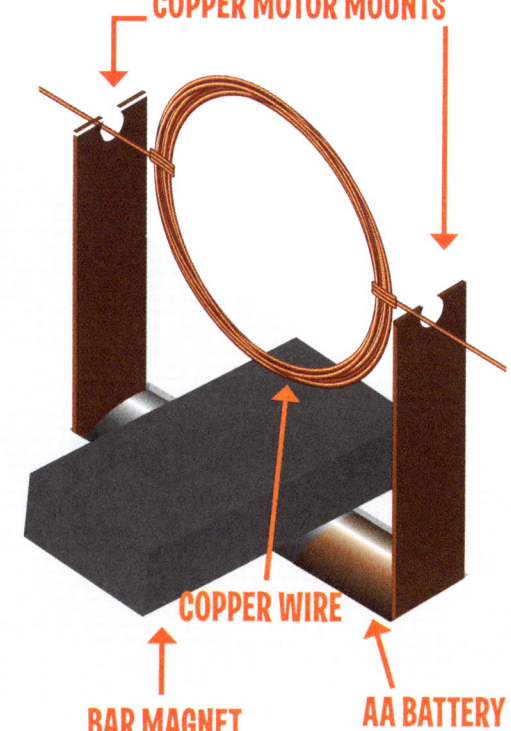

**COPPER MOTOR MOUNTS**

**COPPER WIRE**

**BAR MAGNET**

**AA BATTERY**

## HOW DOES IT WORK?

When the copper motor mounts are connected to the battery and the un-insulated wire coil is touching the motor mounts, a circuit is formed and a current flows through the coil. When the current flows, it becomes an electromagnet and is attracted to the ring magnet below. As the coil spins, the contact is broken when the insulated half of the wire passes the motor mount. Once the coil makes a complete rotation, the circuit is completed again and the coil continues to spin.

31

# FLOATING BOUNCING RING MAGNET

Follow the floating, bouncing magnet and create a cool magnetic toy.

1. Push an unsharpened pencil into the Styrofoam.
2. Slide the ring magnets on the pencil so they repel each other. (Actually the more ring magnets the better.)
3. Now try to push the top magnet down. Let go and see how high the magnet jumps!

**YOU NEED:**
- Unsharpened pencil
- Two ring magnets
- 3" x 3" (7.5cm X 7.5cm) block of Styrofoam

## HOW DOES IT WORK?

Similar poles repel each other. The pencil holds the rings in place. When you push down, the magnet fields repel each other. When you let go, the top magnet jumps away from the bottom magnet.

# FLOATING MAGNET

Ground control...this is Space Flight 9 awaiting your command for launch.

**YOU NEED:**
- Paper airplane
- One bar magnet or ring magnet
- Clear tape
- String

1. Make a paper airplane. Not too big.
2. Tie one end of the string around a paper clip.
3. Tape the paper clip to the plane.
4. Tape the bar magnet to the underside of a shelf on a bookcase.
5. Put the airplane, with paper clip, against the magnet.
6. Gently pull down on the string until the plane floats in mid air.
7. Tape the other end of the string to the bottom shelf.

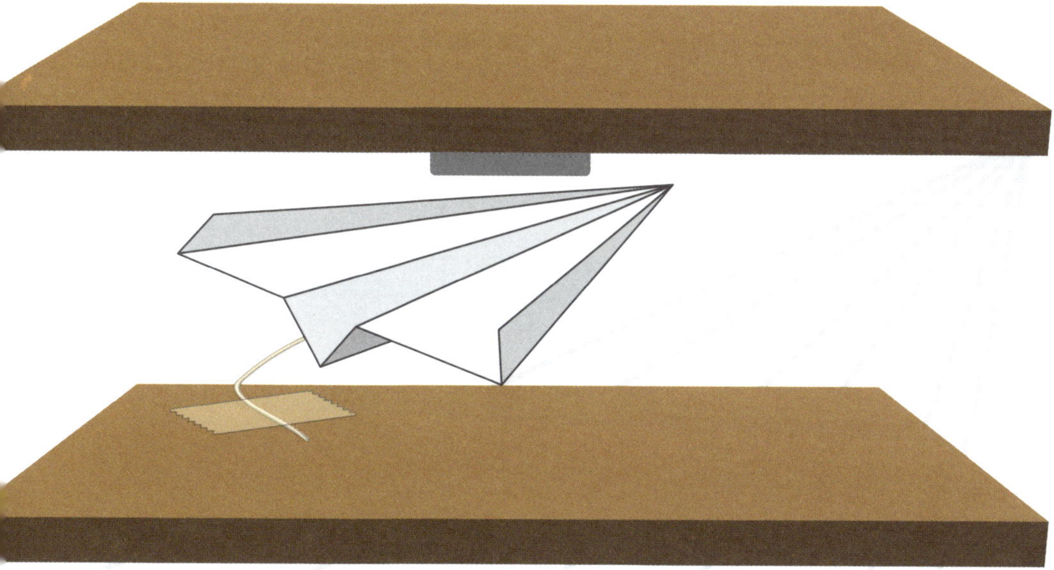

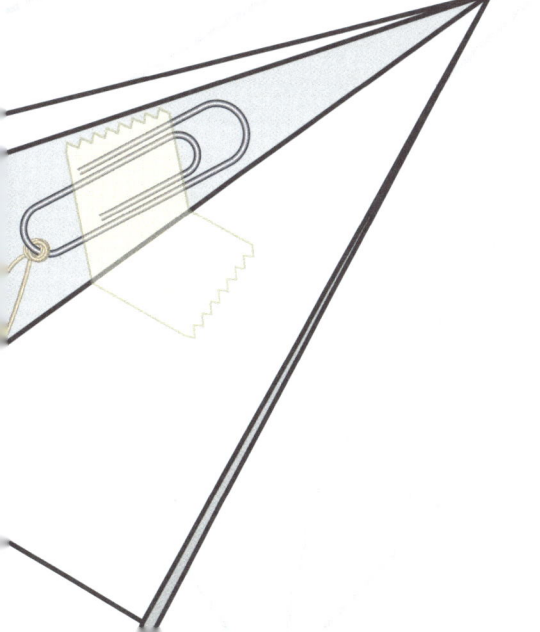

## HOW DOES IT WORK

Since the paper clip is attracted to the magnet and the magnetic field extends out for a small distance, the string holds the plane and paper clip within the magnetic field and it floats.

# AWESOME INVENTIONS

Take a look at this list – what do all these things have in common?

- Refrigerators
- Telephones
- Computers
- VCRs

Stumped? They all need magnets to make them work. And that's just the beginning—the world is full of magnet machines!

MRI machines use magnets to look inside the human body. Maglev trains use magnets to make trains float in midair. Magnets are also used to lift cars in junkyards, to find metal deposits deep underground—and, of course, to attach your annoying little brother's latest drawing to the front of your refrigerator!

So now you've learned a whole lot about magnets and about how powerful and important they are. Of course, there's always more to learn, so check out your local library for more info if you really want to be a magnet master! Who knows, you could be the world's next great inventor!

**WHAT IF YOU WERE GIVEN A MEGA MAGNET, AND ALL THE TOOLS AND MATERIALS YOU NEEDED? WHAT WOULD YOU INVENT?**